The Haunting at Sugar Swamp

Illustrated by
Mary Davis

Dedication:

To the newest member of our family –
Ashton Lilliana Cote.
Born Feb. 24, 2012.
In her the imagination will live on.

Ricky Rebick is a little frog who lives in Sugar Swamp. You might wonder how it got such a name. Grandma Rebick said a long time ago when the wagon trains were traveling west, one broke down in the swamp and a very large bag of sugar spilled into the water.

Grandma would know cause she's pretty old
and knows things like that.

One day Minnie Muskrat came scuttling down the bank to the pond and was all excited about the conversation she heard between nearby farmers, P. T. Brown and Stumpy Smith.

P. T. lives east of the pond and Stumpy lives to the west. Each of them claimed they owned sugar swamp,

but what was so scary, P. T. declared he was going to get his bulldozer out and fill in the place with dirt! This sounded pretty bad to Ricky so he quickly hopped to Mamma frog and asked,

"Mamma, what is a bulldozer?"

She said "I don't know exactly but it's big and noisy. You must ask your Father."

When he went
to Father he said,
"It's a big smoke
spitting creature
with huge
round feet."
This sounded
even worse!

Ollie owl came
swooping down and
landed in his favorite
nearby tree.

When Ricky asked Ollie about
the evil dragon named Bulldozer,
Ollie was amused but also concerned.

He said he would spread the word
about filling in the swamp.

Ollie flew to nearby woods and pastures calling a meeting to save Sugar Swamp.

That Saturday all the creatures began to come in from surrounding farms.

After much discussion, it was decided that a special event was to take place in a week – May fifth to be exact.

The night arrived and a sliver of a moon and a few stars were all you could see.

It was Pitch Black Dark! Suddenly the pond began to glow with an eerie greenish light.

At first, all the animals were afraid and wanted to run away. Ollie Owl called out a big "HOOT" and said, "Do not be afraid. Look closer at the light."

A closer look revealed the source of the light. Every firefly from miles around hovered over the water putting on their brightest lights. It was a sight that could be seen for miles. All the farmers became afraid of the eerie greenish light. Stumpy and P.T made a law that neither of them owned the swamp and they would both leave it alone.

The surrounding farmers steer clear of the swamp and put up a sign saying

DANGER KEEP OUT.

Ricky is older now with a lily pad and family of his own. On the evening of May fifth every year they all gather around the pond to see the magical glow that saved Sugar Swamp.

End

Another book by Murf Chilson is about
life on a farm through the eyes of the animals.
A lovable donkey named Sir Dudley Duncan
Donkey joined with his friends, taking the reader
into the wonderful world of farm animals. Each
of it's five chapters has a lesson to be learned.
Venture with Dudley and his friends around the
farm and even a trip to the beach.

Sir Dudley Duncan Donkey
And His Barnyard Friends